MW01488633

The Collateral Soul

[signature]

Mrs. Elaine Smith

Thanks for your continued support!

1

Tony D. Gunn Jr.

ISBN: 978-1-304-03849-4

The Collateral Soul

Tony D. Gunn Jr.

ACKNOWLEDGEMENTS

I would like to acknowledge my family for all the support they gave me the past year and a half. They surely deserve to be blessed for believing in my abilities to complete this book and to do it well. It is to God, my Lord and Savior, that I owe the utmost respect. It is through His blessings that my family has been able to truly support me through my journey.

Tony D. Gunn Jr.

INDIVIDUAL ACKNOWLEDGEMENTS

Mockia Shelton

-I want to personally thank you "MOM" for supporting me on my books and following my dreams.

Sandra Shaner

-I want to thank you for all your help editing my first book and, now, this one. You have been a great blessing to me.

TABLE OF CONTENTS

6

Chapter 1

Growing up on the North side of Chicago wasn't easy for Darnell Brown. Everyday there was something new to see. It could be bad or good; one thing for sure…it was unexpected. Darnell had a lot of hardships growing up without his father and mother. His mother died from breast cancer when she was 43 and he didn't know his father at all. All he knew about his father was that he named him. And really, that's all he wanted to know.

He ended up living with his Grandmother, which turned out to be very beneficial for support. She made sure that he stuck to his morals and remembered all the knowledge his mother gave him. Darnell Brown always paid attention to everything that was happening around him, but he didn't let that influence him. His mind was focused on his books, getting his CNA Certificate, and his dream of one day having a family. And he promised himself that he would be a better father to his kids than his father was to him.

In his freshman year of college he met a young lady by the name of Linda Palmere. Ms. Palmere and Darnell started dating and surprisingly she became pregnant with Darnell's first child by the end of their senior year. Linda's parents frowned upon having a baby out of wed-lock and Darnell knew his mother did as well, so the marriage was prompt. In the midst of all the immediate planning, Darnell had to think about what he was going to do next to provide for the little girl he was bringing into this world.

The next step Darnell took was attending an accredited phlebotomy program to get his license. Once he obtained his license, he accepted a job as a phlebotomist at a hospital nearby. This was a great start to fulfilling his dream. After the wedding, Mrs. Linda and Darnell purchased a house in Chicago. Soon after, little Amber was born. Amber became the heart of both her parents.

Although Mrs. Linda was the one who stayed home to care for the baby, Darnell held Amber every chance he got.

8

Everything was thought out very well for the first three years of their marriage until another unexpected surprise. Mrs. Linda had become pregnant, again. This was shocking to the both of them, but not upsetting at all. The only thing that bothered them was that they were planning on moving, Darnell was offered a job doing the same thing he been doing, but with a higher pay in Atlanta, GA.

After countless conversations, they decided to continue with the move. Darnell found a nice home in Atlanta, enrolled Amber into the school system and they moved. Comfortably arranged in their new setting, they waited patiently for the arrival of their little boy. All of their family members made a trip down to greet their little boy, Robert Brown, into the world. After the conclusion of this remarkable event, everything went back to normal for the family. Mrs. Linda took care of the two children and Darnell went to work.

Over the next 8 years, things were aligning great. Amber was enrolled into a private school called Bamisqua Academy. She got a scholarship from the school for being a high honor student and playing soccer very well. Robert was enrolled into a public school called Observe the Future. He excels in school too. Mrs. Linda and Darnell

Tony D. Gunn Jr.

hoped he will get a scholarship to a private school when it is his time. No pressure was put on Robert, but the same couldn't be said for Darnell.

His job was stressing him more than it ever had before. Everyone around him were slacking which meant he had to endure an overload of uncommon problems. The nurses were not doing their jobs and on top of that, the hospital had interns there that didn't even know what the job required. It all was frustrating and Darnell ended up leaving work early. Upon his arrival at home, he sat with the car in park mode and tried to calm himself down. The more he tried to calm down the more he thought about the situations at the hospital. In realization of this, Darnell started to think about his kids.

"The kids started summer break this week." thought Darnell, "How could I forget?"

Darnell turned the car off and went inside the house. Once in the house, he was greeted by his wife.

"Hey, how was your day?" asked Mrs. Linda.

"Please, just leave it alone, Linda." replied Darnell, "I don't want to talk about it at all."

Mrs. Linda felt a little offended by his choice of words and, like always, she said something about it.

"Excuse me, don't you come in this house with an attitude! Now I don't know what's wrong with you, but I do know I will not tolerate your disrespect!"

"Hun, I didn't mean anything by it. It's not like that at all" replied Darnell.

"Save it, Darnell!" yelled Mrs. Linda.

Darnell's face turned red. He knew that he wasn't trying to come off as disrespectful, but at the moment, he was pushed into a corner from problems at work and the current situation with his wife, so he reacted.

"Woman, I told you that I didn't mean to seem disrespectful. I've been dealing with problems at work with these ignorant people all day. This is job that pays for your purses and your jewelry and your hair and your nails, so I couldn't quit! I don't have the patience to deal with your bull-crap, too!" yelled Darnell.

A moment of silence struck the room. Tears started to fall from Mrs. Linda's face as she picked up her car keys from

Tony D. Gunn Jr.

the black painted dresser and said, "I'll be damned if I let you talk to me this way."

Then she yelled to the children to put on their jackets. Mrs. Linda and the two kids, Amber and Robert, got into the car. The sounds of clicks from the seatbelts were in the air as Mrs. Linda blasted out of the driveway.

 Amber and Robert slumped close together as fear became the dominant feeling in the atmosphere. They were afraid of how their mom pulled out. Not noticing that she was scaring the kids, Mrs. Linda continued to drive erratically, yet had no idea where she would go. The kids threw frightened looks at each other as she let anger take control of the steering wheel and barely made it through the intersection before the light changed to red.

The accelerator pushed almost to the floor, Mrs. Linda flew down the street. A hundred feet away from another intersection, the light flashed to a flickering yellow as Mrs. Linda gassed it in an attempt to beat the light. The car darted through the wind into the intersection. Time seemed to slow as reality smacked her with a glimpse view of a front bumper before impact. A pick-up truck had slammed into the front of her car causing the kids to rattle in the back seat within the limits of the seat belts and Mrs. Linda to

Tony D. Gunn Jr.

bang her head against the side bar of the door. The car went into a fish-tail and degenerated just before it was about to smack a light pole.

Shredded glass and bent metal poked through the front of the car. Mrs. Linda was lucky that it barely missed her stunned body. The kids' bodies ached, and their eyes remained closed, fearing what lay before them. Some bystanders immediately rushed to the car, while others called the police. No one in the petrified crowd touched the injured family because they didn't know how badly they might be hurt. The police finally arrived on the scene, followed quickly by an ambulance. "Make way! Make Way!" said the first officer on the scene.

Officials rushed through the crowd and tended to the victims. The Paramedics noticed that Mrs. Linda was out cold, so they checked for a pulse.

"She has a pulse!" yelled Paramedic Travis as they carefully used the "Jaws of Life" to cut her from the car and rush her to the hospital.

It was easier to remove the children from the wrecked car and they, too, were taken to the hospital to check out their cuts and scrapes. When they arrived, they were taken to

Tony D. Gunn Jr.

the ER where Dr. Morehead checked them carefully while learning names and their home phone to call their father.

The nagging ring interrupted Darnell from his meal. He picked up the phone and said, "Hello."

"Hello," said Dr. Morehead, "I am a doctor at DMB Hospital, are you the father of Amber and Robert Brown?"

"Yes, how may I help you?" said Darnell with concern.

"Your wife and children were in an automobile accident and she is being treated here at DMB Hospital; your children were shaken up, but they are fine." said Dr. Morehead.

"And my wife, is she okay?" asked Darnell.

"Sir, I would rather not discuss that over the phone." replied Dr. Morehead.

Darnell hung up the phone and rushed out the door. Driving carefully, Darnell still pushed the speed limit and yellow lights at every chance. Bursting through the hospital doors, Darnell was distraught as he looked for someone who could help him find his wife and kids.

Tony D. Gunn Jr.

Dr. Morehead overheard the beginning conversation between Darnell and the hospital security, so she went to the waiting room to get Darnell.

"Come right this way sir, I'm Dr. Morehead." she stated.

"Thank You" said Darnell with slight relief, "My kids, my wife, where are they?"

"One moment Mr. Darnell," said Dr. Morehead, "they're right through these doors."

She took him to see his children before she told him about his wife. Darnell's eyes grew teary at the sight of his children. The kids were still shaken up from the accident and they ran to him, arms opened. Darnell kissed them on their foreheads and told him he was glad they were okay. He let them know he was happy to see them and he was sorry for letting that happen to them. He felt like it was his fault, but he had other things on his mind. Darnell let go of the children, turned to the doctor, and asked "Where's my wife?"

Dr. Morehead responded, "May I speak with you in the hallway?" Darnell and Dr. Morehead left the room. Darnell looked at Dr. Morehead with his overflowing eyes.

Tony D. Gunn Jr.

"I'm sorry, but your wife is in a coma and in critical condition. We're not sure if she is going to wake up anytime soon. The longer she's in the coma, the less positive the outcome may be." said Dr. Morehead.

Darnell dropped to his knees with his hands on his forehead.

"Why, my lord? I know she hasn't been the best, but she doesn't deserve this." Darnell cried out.

Dr. Morehead helped Darnell up to his feet and helped him to a nearby chair. Darnell gathered himself, stood up and asked if he could see his wife. Dr. Morehead led him to Mrs. Linda's cubicle in the ER.

They entered the room and Darnell moved slowly towards her, he felt so guilty. He kissed her cheek and gently held her hands. His eyes overflowed with tears again as he touched her. Dr. Morehead left the room as Darnell began to speak to his wife. He went on-and-on about how sorry he was. He told her that he felt so guilty because the last things he said to her were mean and hurtful. After the confession, Darnell left the room that held his wife and went looking for the room where his children waited.

He saw Dr. Morehead and said, "Is it okay if I have someone come get my kids now?"

Dr. Morehead responded, "Yes, their scrapes have been treated, and they can be released."

Darnell called his sister and told her to come get his kids. His sister felt the tone in Darnell's voice so she didn't hold him up with any questions other than from where and when.

 Darnell went to their waiting area and motioned for them to join him and the children ran out of the room to their dad's arms. Darnell told them to put on their jackets because their great aunt would be arriving to pick them up shortly. The children were still very scared and quietly waited for her to arrive. After she was there, she said a brief prayer for Darnell and his wife, then left with the kids. They got into the car and the distance between them and the hospital grew.

Darnell stayed at the hospital for two days, hoping to be there when his wife emerged from the coma, but there was no change. The doctors explained to him that they would continue to run tests and try to keep her stable, but it was really up to her. She had to have the strength to wake up

Tony D. Gunn Jr.

out of the coma. They suggested that he go home to tend to his kids and they would call him if there was any change in his wife's condition. Since Darnell wanted to be sure his kids were doing as well as they could in the situation, he agreed and left.

He picked the kids up from their aunt's home and they headed home. Darnell wanted to talk to the kids about their mom, but he decided to wait 'til they got home. He constantly looked back at the kids through the rearview mirror.

He wondered how the kids' lives would be affected by this accident and the absence of their mother. Knowing that the kids could lose their mother made him even more depressed, let alone the feeling of potentially losing his wife. They pulled into their driveway and went into the house. Darnell led the kids in the living room and sat them on the couch. He explained to them that their mom had been hurt in the car accident and that everyone at the hospital was working to make her well again.

He left the room and went into the kitchen to make dinner. He wanted to ease their minds so he made their favorites. He made chicken, salad, mashed potatoes, and corn.

Tony D. Gunn Jr.

Seven o'clock p.m. slowly crept on the clock and dinner was finally ready.

Darnell called upstairs to the kids, "Wash your hands and come eat!"

The kids raced to the bathroom, both trying to wash their hands first. Amber made it first because she was the oldest. They walked into the kitchen and smiles curled up their bright faces. They were excited to see all of their favorites on the table waiting for them. The kids thought that since their mother wasn't there, their Dad would only make a sandwich and chips.

They didn't really forget that their mom was in a coma, but they were young and didn't fully feel the same range of emotions as their father. They rushed to their seats and began to eat. Everyone ate quickly and Darnell sent the kids off to bed as he went to his room. He thought about what he went through today; from the arguing to the potential loss of his entire family. Darnell could hardly sleep, but the stress and exhaustion finally won out and he slept.

Tony D. Gunn Jr.

Chapter 2

Two days later, after regular visits to the hospital and calls to his supervisor about the lack of change, he raced to answer the house phone. As he did, he found Dr. Morehead on the other end.

"Good Evening, Mr. Darnell. I was calling because your wife's treatment team would like to meet with you to provide an update on her condition and prognosis."

Darnell told her he was on his way and quickly hung up the phone. The children were ready for bed and he didn't want to disrupt them any more by taking them with him, so he asked a neighbor to come over and get both of them in bed by 8:00 p.m. He got to the hospital quickly and waited for Dr. Morehead or one of the nurses to meet with him.

"Mr. Darnell, I know this has been hard on you these past few days, but you need to know that your wife hasn't regained brain function since she's been here. It's been three days now, and we don't see any likelihood that she would recover." said Nurse Tiarra.

Darnell, realizing how much he had been hoping for a "happy ending", broke down in tears devastated by the news. Nurse Tiarra gave him more details and Darnell drove home with everything the nurse had told him swirling through his mind.

He started to speed up the car behind an eighteen wheeler. He was going to end his life by jamming the car under the back wheels; if he couldn't live it with his wife. "Vroom", the car came about 5 inches from the back of the eighteen wheeler at 55 mph, when suddenly, an image of his children popped into his head. He thought of what his children would suffer if they lost both of their parents. He reminisced about how hard it was growing up without his father, so he could imagine how hard it would be for them growing up without both of their parents. He steered away from the eighteen wheeler truck and safely drove the rest

21

of the way home. Once in the house, he thanked his neighbor then went into his room.

He thought to himself, "Why would the Lord allow this to happen to such an innocent woman?" Darnell knew that the Lord did not cause this, but it was his impulsive thoughts that kept dominating his reasonable thoughts.

His emotions changed from depressed to outrage. He was mad at the God he was raised to believe in; who was supposed to know all, to forgive all and to protect all.

"The Lord will protect you and keep you from all harm! Where is the protection!" said Darnell as he grabbed the Bible from his nightstand and threw it at the wall.

But that didn't quell his anger so he opened his bedroom window and threw the Bible out onto the side walk. Six seconds in the air and the Bible fell in front of a man. Darnell noticed the inconvenient spot the Bible landed in and yelled an apology to him.

"It's okay," said the man, "Looks like I could be just the man you need to see."

"What's that supposed to mean?" responded Darnell curiously.

22

"The Lord gave up on me too. So I turned to the Devil." said the man.

"I lost my wife today and it just feels like my life is falling apart. The last things I said to her certainly didn't do her justice because she was a great person." said Darnell. "I remember when she used to take care of me after I broke my leg playing football. Boy, she never left my side."

"If you come with me, I think I can help you." said the man.

"I can't, man. My kids are here sleeping and I don't have anyone to watch them." replied Darnell.

"Understandable. Take my number down and call me if you change your mind." said the man.

Darnell wrote down the man's number and shut his window. Darnell stayed up a little while longer thinking about everything, and then he went to sleep.

The next morning Darnell woke up with everything still on his mind from last night, but he slightly regretted the extent he exerted it. He was so confused on what to do.

Tony D. Gunn Jr.

"Should I stay faithful to the Lord and let him work it out or should I give up on him and…give in to the devil." thought Darnell.

Eventually, Darnell decided to turn to God one last time before taking this into his own hands. He woke the kids up and got them dressed. Once everyone was ready, they left the house and headed toward their church. Everyone was happy to see the family and was concerned about them. The only problem was that Darnell was tired of hearing everybody say the same thing.

"Everything's going to be alright…everything's going to be alright! I can't take it!" yelled Darnell as he walked back and forth in the bathroom.

While the kids were with their ministry, Darnell decided to go talk to the pastor, one on one, about the situation. He approached the pastor and the conversation started. Darnell kept asking him questions; he was trying to get some kind of understanding of what he was going through. Nothing was adding up to Darnell. He didn't know why God didn't protect his family. After the conversation was over, Darnell still didn't have a clue on what to do. So Darnell resorted back to what he always been told, "You always have options…"

24

After this thought was in Darnell's head, he gathered the kids and left the church. On the way home, he called the neighbor and asked if she could babysit the kids for about two hours. The neighbor agreed and met Darnell at his car to retrieve the kids once he pulled in front of her house. While sitting in front of the neighbor's house, he pulled out the number that the man gave him last night. Darnell started to dial the number, but then he stopped. He questioned if he really wanted to go through with this, but what option was left. He already tried to let God handle it, but nothing happened. Darnell felt like he had no other options, so he typed the rest of the numbers into his phone.

To Darnell, it seemed to take hours for the man to answer the phone, but when he did, they had a conversation. The conversation ended with Darnell preparing to go to the man's trailer home. It started to rain outside and Darnell had heard, while at church, that a storm was passing through today. Darnell started to drive. He saw clouds turn grey as he drove down this long road in the middle of nearby woods. Darnell was scared to keep going, but he felt like he was at a point of no return. Once he arrived at

Tony D. Gunn Jr.

the man's trailer home, he went to knock on the door. As he knocked, the door began to open and Darnell was now face-to-face with the man.

Darnell went into the man's home. Darnell looked all around at the blazing fire red candles and posters of triple six. Fear wrapped around him with every step.

"Have a seat, and let's begin." said the man. Darnell sat in a red painted wooden chair. "Would you like your wife back?" asked the man.

Darnell hesitated to reply. He really didn't know how to answer this strange question, but he answered it.

"Yeah, I would; she's in a coma and the doctors say she isn't gonna' make it." answered Darnell with a mixture of depression and curiosity. He was curious as to how the man plans to fulfil his question.

"How would you feel about selling your soul?" responded the man.

Darnell's eyes opened all the way as he said, "Sell my soul. You can't be serious. I've heard of people doing that, but I never believed it was true!"

Tony D. Gunn Jr.

Then Darnell started to laugh. In his mind, he started to take the man as a joke. He thought the man would have him doing a whole lot of crazy rituals to bring his wife back to full health.

"I'm the most serious person you'll ever meet. If you don't believe in my ability then you can live with the memory of your last conversation with your wife. It's your choice Darnell." said the man.

Darnell sat and thought, again. No matter how many times he thought about what to do, he still came back to one conclusion.

"I'll do whatever it takes to get my wife back." said Darnell.

The man got up from his seat and pulled out a black bag. He placed a red candle at each corner of the desk before drawing a six pointed star in the middle of the desk. Darnell watched as the man prepared for whatever he was about to do. The man grabbed a glass bowl off the floor and made a fire within it. Then he placed an upside down cross in the bowl and held out his hand.

"Take my hand if you want your wife back. All my leader wants in return is your soul." said the man.

Tony D. Gunn Jr.

Darnell hesitated tremendously before placing his hand into the man's hands.

"Close your eyes and hold on tight to my hands. Do not let one finger leave my hands or you'll be damned." said the man.

"Oh beast, I have brought you another one; the soul of a man who realizes your great power. The soul of a man who knows this is his hour. His hour to give his soul to you, oh beast, and all he begs for in return is his shining flower; his wife. He wants good health to enter back into her life. Oh beast, would this be alright?" yelled the man.

The whole trailer home started to shake and rocks and sticks slammed into the walls. Darnell jumped a little, but he did not let the man's hands leave his.

"I called on you, beast, to bring you another soul; a soul of a man who has been betrayed by your enemy; a soul of a man who now realizes your supreme power. All he asks in return is his wife, Linda Brown, to be returned to his family from a coma and you may take his soul for collateral." the man said respectfully.

Suddenly, rocks and sticks from outside the trailer started slamming on the trailer. Loud screeches surrounded them.

Tony D. Gunn Jr.

The man eased the grip on Darnell's hands, but Darnell didn't want to let go. He was too scared of what he had just witnessed. The man said, "Open your eyes and let my hands go. Your request has been granted by our beast."

Darnell slowly released the man's hands as he opened his eyes.

"When will I get to see my wife, again?" asked Darnell.

"Your wife will be returned to you within 48 hours under one further condition, said the man".

"What's that?" asked Darnell.

"Fifty dollars." replied the man.

Darnell looked at the man really strange, now. He noticed the imprint of the man's veins grew bolder the longer Darnell failed to reply. Darnell gave the man the money and left the trailer home without hesitation. When Darnell got home, he paid the neighbor and let her leave. Then he went to check on his kids.

Both of them were still sleep and Darnell went into his room and got ready for bed. Darnell lay down, but couldn't go to sleep because his mind was troubled. The two things

29

that were keeping him from sleep were thoughts of the
future lie he had to give his kids and thoughts of his wife.
He constantly thought of different ways to tell the kids, but
it was harder than he expected. After a while, he finally
thought himself to sleep.

Chapter 3

Three days went by and Darnell was becoming worried. He thought that the man had scammed him for his money. Darnell started to go back into this state of depression, but he didn't want to bring the kids down, so he just hoped for the best. The next morning, Darnell was up preparing a wonderful breakfast. He cooked cinnamon rolls, sausages, bacon, and eggs. He also cut up some strawberries and bananas. After that he divided the meal onto four plates. He looked around and saw that everything turned out right so he ran upstairs to get the children.

"Wake up, daddy's babies." said Darnell with a soft voice as he gently pushed against their backs.

Tony D. Gunn Jr.

The kids woke up with their eyes barely opened and saliva damped around their mouths.

"Breakfast is waiting on you both downstairs." said Darnell with a confident smile.

They both replied with excitement, "Yes!" Darnell's face frowned as he smelled the morning breath aroma leak from his children's mouths.

"Make sure both of you brush your teeth because it stinks." said Darnell.

Laughter filled the room as the kids hopped out of the bed to go to the bathroom. After Darnell made sure that the kids were brushing their teeth, they all went downstairs to eat. They sat down at the table in their normal seats, glancing quickly at their mother's vacant place.

"Can I say the prayer today, daddy?" asked Amber, but Darnell brushed away her offer with:

"Naw baby, It wouldn't be right to bring a blessing forth without your mother's presence. It's not right to continue something we did when mom was here if she is not at the moment." responded Darnell.

"'dn't think of that. Okay dad." said Amber.

Gunn Jr.

They began eating the delicious meal. Amber started to eat when she noticed the plate full of food were her mom use to sit.

"Daddy, *w*hy is that plate there?" said Amber curiously.

Darnell looked at the plate as if he was surprised then looked at her.

"I've been meaning to tell y'all something." said Darnell, "I got a call from Dr. More*h*ead and she had good news. The hospital made a horrible mistake. Mommy is going to recover and will be here at any moment." said Darnell.

The kids began to smile and show gratefulness of the news. By this time, breakfast was over and the kids were nice and full. Darnell cleaned up the kitchen, leaving the untouched plate untouched, and asked the kids if they would like to go see a movie. The kids were very hesitant about answering the question. They wanted to go to the movies, but they didn't want to leave home knowing their mom could be back at any moment.

Tony D. Gunn Jr.

After Darnell did a little persuasion, the kids agreed so they got ready to leave. All of them put on their jackets, locked up the house, and left.

Darnell took the kids to go see a new hit kid movie called "Cars and Planes 15". He bought the kids beverages and snacks of their choice. This was truly a one-on-two bonding experience that Darnell enjoyed. After the movie, Darnell took the kids to a nearby park to burn off some energy. The kids ran around the park playing a variety of games and having a great energetic session. An hour and a half flew by and it was time to return home.

Tony D. Gunn Jr.

Chapter 4

They pulled up to the driveway and got out of the car. As soon as Darnell got in the house he flopped on the living room couch, Bobby went upstairs to his room, and Amber went into the kitchen to get a drink.

"Daddy, Daddy! Come quick! The plate is empty now!" yelled Amber with excitement.

Darnell jumped up off the couch and went into the kitchen. He saw that the plate was empty and immediately ran upstairs. He ran into the kid's room first, but all he saw was Bobby playing the game.

Then he darted to his bedroom and the sight was unbelievable. There she was, sitting on the bed with not a trace of a coma. Seconds later, the kids stormed the room and ran to their mom. They welcomed her back with a flood of hugs and kisses. Then Bobby went on and on about how much they missed her and Amber agreed. Darnell let the kids have their time with her and then sent them to bed.

"Baby I missed you so much. I mean like, I couldn't do anything without thinking of you." said Darnell as he held her.

"I missed you, too, baby, but I don't remember anything. All I really remember is driving...then I got hit! I got hit! Then when I woke, I was in a white endless room. I searched and searched for a way out, but then it turned red as I fell from the room into...I don't know what it was. Maybe a cave or pit? All I know was that it was scary." said Mrs. Linda.

They talked and talked about the situation and shared emotions. Mrs. Linda was the first to get off topic being very sexual, but Darnell rapidly took action. Body to body they both enjoyed each other then went to sleep. The next morning Darnell woke up around 7:00 a.m. to make breakfast. He made the same breakfast as the day before, but this time he switched the cinnamon rolls for blueberry pancakes.

Tony D. Gunn Jr.

He woke everyone when the food was ready and they ate the well balanced breakfast. Darnell went upstairs to get ready for work while Mrs. Linda cleaned up and played with the children. Darnell never once wondered if his wife was mentally stable enough to watch over the children; he was a little curious about how they would do now that she was back, but he was not worried. He kissed his wife and kids bye then left for work.

"Amber take your brother outside in the backyard and play." said Mrs. Linda, "I'll bring out some more toys from the basement."

The kids ran outside as Mrs. Linda went into the basement. She got the toys and went back upstairs. When she approached the back door, all of a sudden her whole mood changed. It was like something snapped in her mind.

"Get in this house now!" yelled Mrs. Linda as she threw the toys on the back porch.

The kids looked at her, fearful and confused, as she repeated herself. With a little hesitation, the kids ran in the house. Mrs. Linda slammed the door with all her might shaking its frame. She pointed them each to different corners of the living room and told them to stay there. The

Tony D. Gunn Jr.

kids sat there with tears running down their faces, heads held down, and brains rattled. They were so confused about what was wrong.

"Mommy can I go to the bathroom?" asked Bobby with fear.

Mrs. Linda got out of her chair and punched him in his back. The impact slammed Bobby's forehead against the wall and he instantly wailed out.

"Leave him alone!" yelled Amber as she started to cry harder.

Mrs. Linda walked over to Amber and slapped her. The slap caused her to hit the side of her head on the wall, leaving her unconscious and motionless.

The angry mom grabbed Bobby by his hair and said, "You better keep this to yourself and not tell your daddy or I'm going to kill him first, then you and your sister!"

She released her grip on Bobby's hair and he fell to the floor.

"Get out of here and go to your room!" yelled Mrs. Linda as he ran away from her and up the stairs.

Tony D. Gunn Jr.

She sat down on the couch and watched TV. Twenty minutes flew by and Amber regained consciousness. Mrs. Linda noticed it and walked over to her. She snatched her up by her hair, grabbed her neck, and slammed her against the wall.

"If your dad finds out what happened today I'm going to kill all of you!" said Mrs. Linda as she tightened her grip on Amber's neck.

Amber gasped for air and strained her neck until Mrs. Linda released her and sat back down on the couch. Amber tried to run toward the steps, but Mrs. Linda ran faster and tripped her. She fell hard to the floor as Mrs. Linda hissed, "Not one word!" Amber got up and ran upstairs to the room. When she got in the room she saw the tears in Bobby's eyes and they hugged each other.

Bobby told her about what happened to him while Amber was unconscious and the threat she made. Amber begged Bobby not to tell their dad about what happened because she was scared for their lives. She didn't know that he was even more scared than she was because he had been afraid that their mother had killed Amber. They sat there and wondered aloud what made their mom act that way.

Tony D. Gunn Jr.

They both came to the conclusion that the accident caused it and that it would wear off eventually.

The kids started to clean up their scratches and torn clothes and calmed down so that their dad wouldn't suspect anything was wrong. Two hours later, Darnell arrived back at home. He went straight to Mrs. Linda and gave her a hug. The kids heard the door shut and they ran downstairs to greet him. As Darnell turned toward the kids Mrs. Linda gave the kids an evil look warning them of their consequences. The kids hugged him as if he had been gone for years.

"Aw, I love you guys, too." said Darnell.

Mrs. Linda went in the kitchen to prepare dinner while the kids and Darnell went into the living room and played a game. Mrs. Linda cooked fried chicken, mashed potatoes, corn, and peas. Then she called them into the kitchen to eat. They all sat there and ate the food. After they were finished everyone went into their bedrooms to prepare for the night. As Darnell was taking off his clothes, the phone rang and he answered it.

"Hi, this is Dr. Morehead calling from DMB Hospital. The duty nurse heard a change in the machines monitoring your wife's conditions and, when she went to check on her, she saw her sitting on the side of the bed removing the connections to the machines. The nurse ran to get a doctor and by the time she returned, your wife was gone. We searched the hospital and eventually checked the security cameras and saw her just walk out."

"Yes, she's here at home. It's a miracle and I was shocked when I saw her. She doesn't have any big sign of ever being in a coma. It's like everything...disappeared!" said Darnell as if he didn't remember what he did to get her back.

"I couldn't believe it when they told me. I need you to get her here for testing as soon as possible." said Dr. Morehead.

"I know! I couldn't believe it myself and I will get her to you all first thing in the morning." said Darnell.

"Okay, that's great! I would like to get some testing done on her right away." said Dr. Morehead.

"I will get her to you as soon as possible." said Darnell as he hung up the phone and got in the bed.

"Who was that?" asked Mrs. Linda.

Tony D. Gunn Jr.

"Just the doctor wondering about you, but everything is okay." replied Darnell.

They talked about the kids and their next school year for awhile before they went to sleep. Mrs. Linda went to sleep first. Darnell had stayed up a little while longer pessimistically thinking more about the possible outcomes of him taking his wife to the hospital in the morning. So he decided not to take her and off to sleep he went.

The next morning Darnell started to get up to make breakfast when he noticed his wife wasn't in the bed. He jumped up and ran downstairs to look for her. He had thought that for some reason that she was gone. When he got to the bottom of the stairs he heard the water running in the kitchen. He ran to the kitchen and was pleased about what he saw. Mrs. Linda was cooking breakfast for them and it smelled good. Darnell walked over to her and hugged her from the back.

Tony D. Gunn Jr.

Chapter 5

"Good morning, baby." said Mrs. Linda as she smiled and laid her head backward against Darnell's shoulder.

Darnell replied, "Good morning baby. It sure does smell good in here."

"Thanks, ba*b*e, but it's going to taste twice as good." said Mrs. Linda.

Darnell released his arms from around her and went to go wake up the kids. Mrs. Linda wasn't too worried about the kids trying to speak of the situation that occurred the day before because she was sure they feared her potential threats. She made all their plates and placed them on the table. She felt confident that Darnell didn't have a clue and wouldn't get any from the kids.

Mrs. Linda's actions were far from over and were progressively getting more violent. She realized that Darnell didn't even notice the bruises on the kids, which made her more confident in her next actions. The food on the table appeared to be perfectly normal, but two of those plates were not edible. She purposely put a little ipecac syrup in the kid's food. Darnell and the kids finally came down and approached the table. They all sat down exactly where Mrs. Linda expected them to.

"The meal looks wonderful honey!" said Darnell.

They all began to eat. Piece by piece Amber and Bobby ate their tampered meals. Once the meal was finished, Darnell left out for work.

"I'll see you all later and if the kids go outside dress them lightly because it's blazing hot." said Darnell.

"That summer weather is crazy, baby." said Mrs. Linda with a grin on her face.

The kids were in the living room on the couch. They thought if they stayed together and completely out of Mrs. Linda's way then she would not bother them. They were very wrong!

Tony D. Gunn Jr.

"Get up and go put on some clothes to go play outside!" yelled Mrs. Linda.

They kids scattered up the stairs to their rooms. Mrs. Linda was right behind them. She directed them to put on three long-sleeve shirts, a pair of shorts, a pair of pants over the shorts, two pairs of socks, and some boots. The kids were aware that it was summer, but they just thought it got cold outside. They all went down stairs to go out the back door into the yard. When they reached the hallway, Mrs. Linda threw them some hats. The kids put them on as Mrs. Linda opened the back door.

The hot summer *air* rushed the kids as they wondered why they had on all those clothes, but they were afraid to say anything. The kids ran off the patio to play as Mrs. Linda sat in the shaded area of the patio in a tank-top drinking iced tea. Five minutes went by and the kids started to overheat. Bobby started to take off his hat and Mrs. Linda saw him. Wham! Bobby flew to the ground stunned and confused about what he did.

"Don't take off anything or else!" yelled Mrs. Linda.

Tony D. Gunn Jr.

Their play time went from fun to terror. Mrs. Linda went back on the patio and resumed her rest. Amber whispered softly to Bobby trying to comfort him.

"It's hot out here, I just wanted to take off some of my clothes." whispering Bobby with a chopped voice.

"I know bro, it'll be okay. Just get up before she says something." said Amber in a very concerned voice.

Bobby got up off the ground and wiped his face off. Their faces showed pure panic, but Mrs. Linda didn't care. It was as if she was desensitized by an unknown force.

"I want both of y'all to run up and down the yard until I tell you to stop. Now!" yelled Mrs. Linda.

The kids took off, quickly becoming exhausted and overheated. Two laps, three laps, four laps, each one adding on to their already overbearing fatigue.

"I can't breathe, I can't breathe." said Bobby as he fainted to the ground.

Smack! Bobby hit the ground head first. Amber stopped instantly to go to the aid of her brother.

Tony D. Gunn Jr.

"Keep running, Ass!" blurted Mrs. Linda as she rose from her seat.

Amber got up and took off so that she would not get attacked. Fear rushed through the body of Amber, but she didn't show it. She knew that showing her fear would only encourage her mom. Mrs. Linda smacked Bobby in the face a couple of times then checked his pulse to make sure he was still alive. She grabbed him up by his hair and threw him over her shoulder. They went into the house and she placed him in the living room. When she went back out, she noticed that Amber had passed out too.

Mrs. Linda grabbed her by her hair and dragged her up the patio stairs. Constant banging of Amber's head on the stairs would ensure a headache when she awoke. Mrs. Linda tossed her on the couch with her brother and left the room. She was going to get a fan and some water. She plugged the fan up and turned it on them. One by one she threw Styrofoam cups of water as hard as she could toward their faces. It took a cup count of four to Bobby's face and nine to Amber's face 'til they awoke.

"Go dry off and clean the Hell up! And don't forget about the consequence of letting our secret get out!" warned Mrs. Linda.

Tony D. Gunn Jr.

The kids got up from the couch scared and fearful of her presence. They ran up stairs to do what she said.

"We have to tell daddy. We have to." whispered Amber fearfully.

"No! No! Please no sis. I don't want anything bad to happen." cried Bobby.

"Something bad has already happened. I don't know how mom is still alive and I don't know why she's acting like this, but this has to come to an end." explained Amber.

"Just hold off on that, sis. We will tell the truth, but we have to be smart about this." said Bobby.

They dried themselves off with a towel as they thought of what had happened. Tears ran down their faces, but they managed to stay quiet. They had learned by now that crying loudly would only give Mrs. Linda a reason to abuse them more. Amber held Bobby in her arms as she started to speak.

"Let's watch TV and try to get it off our minds." said Amber as she turned on the TV.

Meanwhile, Mrs. Linda was downstairs cleaning up so nobody would suspect what she'd done. She knew any seemingly unrelated question, such as about water over the couch, could led to her story unraveling. She put fans directly in front of the couch as she dried the floors.

Tony D. Gunn Jr.

Chapter 6

A hour passed and Darnell came home after his work day.

"I'm home, baby." said Darnell to Mrs. Linda as she ran to the back of the house to store the fans.

"I'm back here, baby, here I come." said Mrs. Linda.

She walked back toward the living room and jumped into Darnell's arms.

"Woo baby, nice to see you, too!" said Darnell with a sexually aroused smile on his face.

"How about after dinner, when the kids go to sleep, we have a little fun?" said Mrs. Linda.

Tony D. Gunn Jr.

"That sounds like a plan, baby." said Darnell as he took off his jacket.

Mrs. Linda headed to the kitchen to start dinner and clear her mind to get prepared for tonight. Darnell went up the stairs to the kids' rooms, but he didn't notice the damp stairs. He opened the door and the kids turned toward him.

"Daddy!" said the kids as they ran to him.

"I love my family." thought Darnell as a reaction to all the love he got when he arrived home. "I miss you guys, too." replied Darnell. "Daddy I have to tell you something." said Amber nervously.

Bobby looked at Amber with worried eyes as Darnell said, "What's up?"

She knew that Bobby's look was a warning, so she thought of a different question.

"Can we get ice cream after dinner?" said Amber.

"Sure, baby." stated Darnell. "Well, dinner will be ready in a little, so I'll see y'all then." said Darnell as he left the room.

Tony D. Gunn Jr.

"Why would you think about telling what she did to us? You know what would happen if you did that. Do you want us both to die?" asked Bobby.

"No, I'm sorry. I was just so happy to see dad that I almost blurted out everything to him." said Amber.

"Please, sis. You have to try to keep it together. I don't want anyone to get hurt." said Bobby as he turned his attention back to the TV.

Bobby and Amber sat down in front of the TV and they both appeared to be watching it even though they were really thinking about what was happening in the house. Moments later, dinner was ready.

"Bobby...Amber...dinner is ready!" pleasantly yelled Darnell from the lower level.

The kids hopped up and headed down stairs.

"Ouch!" said Bobby as he clenched to his stomach.

"What's wrong?" asked Amber while their parents rushed to the stairs.

"My stomach hurts!" cried Bobby as Darnell wrapped his arms around him.

Tony D. Gunn Jr.

"He must have eaten too much this morning and the smell from dinner just triggered this." said Mrs. Linda.

"You'll be fine." said Darnell as he picked Bobby up and took him up stairs to lay him down.

When Darnell got all the way upstairs, Mrs. Linda grabbed Amber by her collar and took her into the kitchen. "Ouch." quietly moaned Amber right before Mrs. Linda elbowed her in the chin.

"Shut up and listen, stupid," said Mrs. Linda," I'm the reason his stomach is hurting, you little pest. Yours should be hurting too, but I guess some get lucky. Now go sit down at the table!"

Mrs. Linda released Amber's shirt and pushed her aside. Darnell came downstairs, grabbed Bobby's plate and put it into the refrigerator. The remaining three family members took a seat at the table. They quietly ate dinner and Darnell was a little troubled by that.

"Why so quiet?" curiously asked Darnell.

"We're just a little tired, baby, but how was your day?" said Mrs. Linda purposely trying to divert Darnell from asking more questions.

Tony D. Gunn Jr.

"Oh, it was alright. And I'm tired, too." said Darnell as he finished the last of his food.

As soon as Amber saw her father rise from the table, she took one last mouthful and got up right behind him. They both left the kitchen when suddenly Amber threw up all over the hallway floor.

"My stomach!" yelled Amber as she dropped to the floor and fell face flat into the vomit.

"Poor baby, maybe you shouldn't have taken that last bite. You stuffed yourself, like your brother." said Mrs. Linda as she helped Amber off the floor and up the stairs.

"You'll be okay baby. It's just an upset tummy. Sleep it off, hon." explained Darnell. Mrs. Linda tossed Amber into her bed.

"See you later." said Mrs. Linda as she closed the door.

Mrs. Linda went down stairs and got on the couch with Darnell. They cuddled and watched a movie. Upstairs, Bobby and Amber were talking.

"She's the reason why our stomachs are hurting." said Amber.

Tony D. Gunn Jr.

"I knew she had something to do with it! I can usually eat a whole lot of food without my stomach hurting." said Bobby.

"It'll be okay 'Lil bro. We got to get away from this. It can't keep happening." said Amber with determination.

Then they watched cartoons until they went to sleep. When their movie was over, Darnell and Mrs. Linda went upstairs.

They checked to see if the kids were asleep and went into their room. Mrs. Linda immediately ripped off her clothes and jumped into the bed.

"Awwww Yeah." said Darnell as he took off his clothes.

They whispered things in each other's ears to arouse their emotions. After intercourse occurred, they went to sleep.

Tony D. Gunn Jr.

Chapter 7

In the morning, Darnell and Mrs. Linda woke up, took their showers and got dressed. Then they headed toward the children's room. Mrs. Linda started to wake the children until Darnell stopped her.

"Let them sleep a while longer. They need to sleep that stomach sickness off." said Darnell.

"You're right, I forgot all about it." replied Mrs. Linda.

They grabbed each other's' hand and headed downstairs. Once downstairs, they went into the kitchen.

"Baby, you cooking or I'm cooking?" asked Mrs. Linda.

"It's up to you, hon." replied Darnell. "I really don't mind either way."

Tony D. Gunn Jr.

"Okay, I will cook then." stated Mrs. Linda.

She started to take out what she was going to cook, and then she stopped. She started to think of how great it would be to watch the kids suffer the pains of their sickness. And this could only happen if Darnell left now so she could wake the kids.

"Baby, you know what? I really don't even feel like cooking or eating a big breakfast today. Can we just eat some of these muffins?" asked Mrs. Linda.

"Yea baby, we can do that." replied Darnell.

She tossed him a banana nut muffin as he started to speak.

"Baby, how you knew this the kind I like?" said Darnell with a chuckle.

"Hon, you always get the banana nut muffin. I'm starting to think you like nuts in your mouth" replied Mrs. Linda.

"Ha ha, you got jokes? But I'm about to head out. I'll see you when I get home." said Darnell.

Tony D. Gunn Jr.

He walked over to her and gave her a smooch on the cheek. She smiled at him and they exchanged those three magical words, I Love You. After locking the door, she walked over to the window and patiently watched Darnell get into the car and drive off. Now that he was out of the picture she could fulfill her plans.

Mrs. Linda went upstairs to the kids' room. She stood in the door way and all of a sudden she yelled at the top of her lungs, "Get up!"

The children awoke in fear and confusion. Bobby ran over to Amber's bed and jumped into her arms.

"Now stay up or I'll give you a memory you won't forget!" said Mrs. Linda as she left the room.

"Promise me something, sis?" cried Bobby, "Promise me you will never speak of telling again?"

"I promise, I promise!" cried out Amber.

Meanwhile, downstairs in the living room, Mrs. Linda knew she had put more than enough fear into the children. She knew they were upstairs in pain and in fear. Every hour or so Mrs. Linda would go yell at the kids and remind them to stay awake.

Tony D. Gunn Jr.

"Well, it's time to get dinner started." thought Mrs. Linda as she went into the kitchen and prepared it. The clock's hour hand creeped to 5:00 p.m. as Darnell walked through the door.

"Umm huh, something smells good!" said Darnell as he closed his eyes and inhaled the tasty aroma. Mrs. Linda put down the spoon she was stirring the mashed potatoes with and ran into Darnell's arms.

"Baby, you know I got you!" said Mrs. Linda with a smile.

The children heard the bits of the conversation as it drifted through the air into their ears. They ran downstairs and simultaneously hugged their father.

"Dad we miss you!" said Amber.

"Aw that's sweet babe...Hey, go get dressed. I'm about to take y'all to the park." said Darnell.

Smiles appeared on the kids' faces as they ran to get dressed.

"You want to go, baby?" asked Darnell.

Tony D. Gunn Jr.

Mrs. Linda briefly thought that she should go because the chance of the kids telling, but she figured the kids were too scared to speak out about it.

"Not really, I got some work to catch up on." said Mrs. Linda.

Darnell gave her a kiss as he went upstairs to take off his work clothes. A few minutes passed by and everyone was ready to go.

"Bye, baby!" yelled Darnell as they left.

The three of them got into the car and headed to the park. Darnell glanced back at the children while he was driving to make sure they had their seat belts on; they did. After ten minutes, they arrived at the park as anticipated.

"Bet I can beat you to the swing!" said Bobby as he got a head-start toward the swing set.

"You cheating, you cheating!" yelled Amber as she easily caught up with him.

"Be careful children." said Darnell as he chuckled a little.

Amber jumped onto one of the swings first, leaving Bobby with a defeat to manage.

"I let you win. I totally could of beat you, but you a girl, so I didn't." said Bobby as he hopped onto the other swing.

"Yea right, sure you did." said Amber sarcastically.

They swung for fun for about 5 minutes, but Bobby started to feel competitive again.

"I bet I can go higher than you." said Bobby, "This time I won't let you win."

"You're on!" yelled Amber as she thrust the swing back-and-forth.

Bobby had a little trick up his sleeve that he had learnt from one of his classmates. He knew that Amber didn't know how to do it because he was secretly studying her swinging form before he opened his mouth about a race to the top.

The only thing Amber had on Bobby was weight, but he knew that the weight advantage would soon be useless. Finally, Bobby passed her up and she was amazed that he was actually going to beat her at something.

Tony D. Gunn Jr.

"I win!" yelled Bobby.

All the excitement flowed through Bobby as his fist pumped as he swung to his limit. Big mistake! Bobby slid off the swing and crashed to the ground.

"Daddy, Daddy!" yelled Amber as she ran to aid Bobby.

She saw the blood and slowly moved back from him. She could not stand the site of blood, and she knew if she looked at it a few more seconds that she would hurl all over Bobby. Darnell ran over to Bobby and notice that the blood came from a little cut on Bobby's forearm.

"You okay?" asked Darnell.

"Yes, I'm fine, daddy. It just stings a little." said Robert.

Darnell asked them both if they were ready to go home and they said no. Robert got up off of the ground and sat on the bench. Amber followed him to the bench. They sat there and watched the other kids play, then noticed something they did not have; their mom. They noticed a couple of kids playing with their moms: the smiles, the laughter, the fun! Amber and Robert felt sad from seeing it and just wanted to go home and get in the bed.

Tony D. Gunn Jr.

"Let's go." said Amber as they both headed toward the car.

Darnell noticed the children heading to the car, so he caught up to them. They got *i*nto the car and left for home. Mrs. Linda heard her family's arrival and went to open the door.

"How was the park?" asked Mrs. Linda.

"It was great!" replied Bobby even though he wanted to ignore her.

She kissed Darnell on the check as he closed the house door.

"Dinner is on the table." said Mrs. Linda.

They went into the kitchen and sat at the table. Everything looked so good, but smelt so much better. Munch, crunch, munch. They all ate their portions of the meal and headed to *t*heir rooms as usual. Neither Mrs. Linda nor Darnell immediately wash the dishes after eating. Both of them were tired and just wanted to lie down. Everyone in the house, except Mrs. Linda was finally asleep. She couldn't stop thinking about what to do next. Eventually her sinister thoughts came to an end and she nodded off, too.

Tony D. Gunn Jr.

Chapter 8

8:00 a.m. Breakfast begun and ended as usual. Everyone was fed and full by the time Darnell left for work. The kids sat at the table as they watched their dad walk out the door. Part of them wanted to just yell out the truth and hope for the best, but the dominant emotion of fear within them made them bite their tongues.

"Go upstairs to your room and watch TV. Don't come out of that room unless I tell you to." informed Mrs. Linda.

The children did what they were told without any hesitation. Hesitation equaled consequence, consequence equaled abuse, and abuse equaled pain: the kids were not stupid. Mrs. Linda started to get the materials for her premeditated plan. She noticed last night that Robert had an open wound, but she didn't say anything about it. She went into

64

the bath room and got some alcohol and a tile. Mrs. Linda knew that the alcohol would help the wound but it would also hurt Robert, especially by the time she finished with it. She sat the alcohol and tile on the kitchen table.

"Come here Robert!" she yelled from the bottom of the stairs.

Robert heard the call and looked to Amber with fear. His mind raced to find something he had did wrong, but he couldn't.

"It'll be okay." whispered Amber as she watched Robert walk out of the room.

She felt a similar feeling watching Robert walk out of the room as when she watched he dad walk out. Robert went downstairs and was guided into the kitchen by his mother. He noticed the alcohol and tile sitting on the table and felt the fear leave his body. He thought she was about to treat his wound like she did before she had her accident. Mrs. Linda grabbed a steak knife out of the dish rack and walked over to Robert as he sat down.

"I need you to be very still." requested Mrs. Linda.

Tony D. Gunn Jr.

She cut the wound open some more with the knife. She wanted the alcohol to really burn because she knew it would weaken him. She wanted to see him cry. Robert yelled out as the blade sliced through his fragile skin as if it was butter. Mrs. Linda laughed while he cried and whispered as she opened the alcohol. She grabbed his wrist tightly and watched the tears compete to fall off his face. "Splash!" Mrs. Linda drenched Robert's arm with alcohol.

The sizzling scared Robert; he thought his arm was going to burn right off. Mrs. Linda commanded him to suck up the pain and be quiet. She put two band-aids on the wound now that it was over twice its previous size.

"Go back upstairs and don't come out!" yelled Mrs. Linda.

Robert ran for the stairs as he held his arm in pain. The pain was overwhelming and he couldn't hold the crying in any longer. He whimpered quietly with every step.

"What's wrong?" asked Amber as Robert staggered through the door.

"I don't want to talk about this." cried Bobby as Amber held him in her arms.

Tony D. Gunn Jr.

Amber sat there rubbing Bobby's back as she got more and more upset. She knew this had to end. Neither of them could take any more physical pain let alone emotional pain of being tortured by their mother. But there wasn't anything she could do that wouldn't eventually risk more pain. Her patience ticked down like a stopwatch in every moment. Meanwhile, Mrs. Linda was downstairs cleaning the alcohol off the floor and re-shelving the alcohol. When she was finished, she sat down in the living room and watched TV. She clicked through the channels searching for something to watch.

She had found a channel that was showing some rather venereal thing*s*. Her estrogens and progesterone were active, but her partner wasn't home from work yet.

"Robert!" yelled Mrs. Linda from the couch.

Robert looked at Amber and this time he hesitated to go, but he had no choice. Amber sat there mad at herself because there was nothing she could do. Robert walked down the stairs wondering what painful horrors were waiting on his arrival. Robert entered the living room and stopped in front of Mrs. Linda as she changed the channel.

Tony D. Gunn Jr.

"Come, sit down." said Mrs. Linda with a soft voice as she patted to a spot close to her.

Robert sat down out of fear, but he didn't know what to fear yet. Mrs. Linda leaned over, grabbed Robert's right hand and place it on her lap. She looked Robert in the eyes and said, "I own you. You do as I say."

Then she leaned in to kiss him. Their lips overlapped, but Robert was still in fear. It took him a few seconds to realize what his mom just did to him. Robert didn't know much about what was going on, but he knew it was wrong. He pulled his head back as Mrs. Linda closed her eyes.

"Pow!" Mrs. Linda punched Robert in the leg and told him not to ever pull away from her again. Robert was scared out of his mind, but he knew one more disobedient stunt like when he pulled a second ago and he was toast.

"Come on, it's time for a nap." said Mrs. Linda as she guided Bobby upstairs to her room.

Amber heard them coming upstairs, so she put the cover over her head and pretended that she was sleep. Footsteps flapped past the kid's room door and into the Mrs. Linda's bedroom. She sat Robert on the bed and gripped his arm tightly. She warned him that if he told

68

anybody, including his sister, about what just happened she'd kill them all. She covered Robert with the cover, closed the door, and left him in there to fall into a troubled sleep. Robert lay there in bed with his brain over worked from trying to comprehend what his mother just did to him. He had never imaged that something like this would happen to him.

"I've seen this before." thought Robert.

Robert had realized that he seen something happen like this on his favorite TV show "Special Victim Department". He kept digging through his brain trying to remember how the victims of that situation handled it. Eventually Robert dozed off. Amber sat in her room thinking of all the horrible things that Mrs. Linda could have done to him.

"She probably cutoff his finger or put a toothpick in his eye." murmured Amber.

The more she imagined horrible scenes, the more she knew that she had to find a way to help him.

Amber listened carefully to try to locate Mrs. Linda. She heard changing of channels downstairs in the living room, so she knew that Mrs. Linda was not upstairs. Amber tried to open the door as slowly and quietly as possible, but the

Tony D. Gunn Jr.

rusty hinges betrayed her. Amber got nervous and wanted to abort her mission, but decided it was worth the risk. She opened the door just enough to squeeze through, then headed toward her parent's room.

Amber opened the door and saw Robert lying in bed motionless. She started to get even more nervous with every foot step toward him. She thought Robert was lying there dead; breathless. She put her hand on Robert's left shoulder and gently rocked him. With the first couple of rocks Robert didn't budge, so she rocked him again just a little harder. Robert, in a deep sleep, murmured to whoever was touching him to leave him alone.

Fear slid off of Amber's shoulders as she realized Robert was okay. Amber left the room with small satisfaction: at least he was still alive. She tip-toed her way toward her room and listened carefully to her surroundings. She thought to herself that she was surely going to get caught, but hoped for the best. Amber focused her eyes on the stairs as she went into her room backwards. She shut the door and gasped while still holding the door knob.

Amber turned around and was frightened by what she saw. Mrs. Linda was sitting on her bed as a man would sit with legs crossed and her hands *t*ogether.

Tony D. Gunn Jr.

"Sneaking out of your room, huh? You lying, untrustworthy little butt! Come here!" said Mrs. Linda as she snatched at Amber and drew the girl to her.

She pinned Amber down on the floor and went on-and-on about how she felt about Amber.

"I'm going to show you what I think about untrustworthy pest!" yelled Mrs. Linda as she grabbed Amber's hair.

She fumbled her fingers through Amber's hair until she reached a few in the middle. Mrs. Linda started to pluck a hair from Amber's head each time she recited the letters that spelled untrustworthy, a total of thirteen hairs.

Amber cried in agony with every pluck. She wiggled and wiggled, but she was no match for Mrs. Linda's size and/ or strength. She got off of Amber and warned her to stay in her place for now on because her next out-break will be her last. Amber nodded her head in desperate agreement as she crawled over to her bed.

Mrs. Linda left the room and descended downstairs to the living room. The entire house was quiet except of the living

Tony D. Gunn Jr.

room TV. Robert was asleep and eventually Amber dozed off too. After Mrs. Linda's show ended, she got up from the couch to go in the kitchen. Before she could get there, she noticed that a new episode was about to start. She wanted to sit back down and watch, but she knew what having dinner ready when Darnell got home meant to him.

So she proceeded into the kitchen and started to think about what she was going to cook. A refrigerator full of food meant that she had a lot of options. And the more options, the harder the choice. So she decided to just go with what she had a taste for: baked chicken, stuffing, and green beans! She got out all the cooking supplies and started on the meal. Dinner time rode around and Darnell was home. The kids were already at the table by the time Darnell actually entered the house.

He kicked off his shoes and greeted his family with hugs and smooches. They all sat at the table and started to eat. Darnell struck up a conversation with the kids because he noticed that they were not smiling or annoying each other and it felt kind of awkward. The kids didn't join in the conversation until Mrs. Linda gave them a mean look that escaped Darnell's notice.

Tony D. Gunn Jr.

"How about after dinner, we all play a board game?" ask Darnell.

The kids nodded their heads happily and there were smiles all around. The kids sat up straight in their seats and started to eat a little faster. They were excited about finally having a little fun. Mrs. Linda put a smile on her face as if she was happy about the upcoming arrangement. Dinner wrapped up and everyone, except Mrs. Linda, headed toward the living room.

"Aren't you going to play with us, baby?" asked Darnell.

"Baby, go ahead. I have to wash these dishes and clean the kitchen." replied Mrs. Linda.

"Okay, baby" said Darnell as he fluttered his tongue.

Mrs. Linda smiled at Darnell then started on the dishes. Darnell went into the hall closet and got a board game to play. The kids were excited about playing the game because that's not what they usually did. They usually went to their room after dinner and watched TV 'til they fell asleep. The game with on for hours and it seemed like it would never end, yet the children kept playing. After about two and a half hours, Darnell finally called it a night.

Tony D. Gunn Jr.

"We will pick this up another day. It's getting late and you all have school tomorrow." said Darnell.

The kids started to laugh; they thought he was joking. "We don't have school tomorrow. We're on summer vacation!" replied Amber as she rolled the dice.

"I meant to say that I have work tomorrow and I have to get to sleep. I promise we will finish this game. Promise!" said Darnell as he hopped up and directed them to take a picture of the game board and put the game away.

The kids did as they were told then headed to their room. Robert ran up the stairs as fast as he could. He wanted to be the first in the room so that he could put the TV on what he wanted to watch for the night. He got what he wanted and when Amber came in, she didn't argue with what he wanted to watch. She just wanted to go to sleep anyway. Although she was the first to fall asleep, Robert wasn't too far behind her.

Over in Darnell and Mrs. Linda's room, they were just began their night. Mrs. Linda had been waiting a little over an hour for Darnell to get upstairs. Once upstairs, they had intercourse.

74

Tony D. Gunn Jr.

Finally, both of them were satisfied and were off to the tub. Darnell took a shower first because Mrs. Linda was too tired to move; her body ached and needed some rest. After Darnell got out of the shower, Mrs. Linda was in a deep sleep and he didn't want to wake her. So, he lay next to her and went to sleep.

Tony D. Gunn Jr.

Chapter 9

The next morning Darnell playfully mocked the sounds and actions of Mrs. Linda from the previous night. They laughed and bumped into each other as they headed to the kitchen. Darnell decided he was going to cook breakfast and Mrs. Linda was fine with that. She needed time to think of what she was going to do to the kids today. She sat in the living room and went into a deep thought.

"Umm, I got it." thought Mrs. Linda as she came to a conclusion.

She hopped up from the couch and went into the kitchen to see Darnell's progress with breakfast. By this time, he already had the plates loaded with the food. The fluffy buttered pancakes were covered in freshly sliced

Tony D. Gunn Jr.

strawberries and were accompanied by some sizzling sausages and sunny-side up eggs. Mrs. Linda drooled at the sight and smell of all that delicious food. While Darnell was cooking the last sausage, Mrs. Linda softly hugged him from the back and kissed the back of his head. Darnell smiled and they exchanged three special words; I love you.

Meanwhile, Amber was awakened by the smell of the food, but she didn't get up. She lay there thinking about her dream that all of this was over and that there were no more beatings to be endured and hidden.

She dreamed that her home was peaceful and everyone in the family was enjoying life. In her dream her mother was gone; she started wondering how she could make the dream real. She was too small to fight and didn't know anyone she could tell even if she wasn't too scared to break the silence. Then an idea hit her.

"Cameras!" thought Amber, "That will help me catch her."

Amber got out of bed and went into the bottom drawer of her dresser. Way in the back of the dresser was a gift card she had got for her birthday from her Aunt J. Her Aunt J passed away a few years ago due to an illness and Amber was very devastated about it.

Amber grabbed the gift card and tip-toed to the computer room. She made it without catching the attention of anyone in the house. Finally, Amber thought she was accomplishing something. She logged onto the desktop and searched for small spy cameras for sale.

"Bingo." whispered Amber as she added the spy cameras to her cart.

Amber had purchased fifteen spy cameras and paid for Next-Day shipping so that she could have the cameras within the next two business days. After purchasing the cameras, she deleted the search history so that no one would know what she had been doing and logged off.

"Kids!" yelled Mrs. Linda.

Amber jumped up in fear. She thought Mrs. Linda had noticed that she was in the computer room. When she realized she was safe, she ran to their room and woke up Robert.

"Breakfast is ready!" finished Mrs. Linda.

Tony D. Gunn Jr.

Amber was relieved when she realized that Mrs. Linda only called them to say that breakfast was ready. The kids headed downstairs. Once again, the family sat around the table and ate, but Amber kept fidgeting: she was even more scared now that she had taken action to stop her mother's abuse. Somehow it was easier just being victimized than taking steps to end it.

She tried her hardest not to show her nervousness. She didn't want to raise any suspicions because she knew that would result in another beating. As usual, Darnell finished first and left for work. By the time Darnell left, the kids were upstairs watching TV, with their door closed. Darnell wondered why the kids didn't see him out, but he just ignored it and went on with his day.

For the next two days Mrs. Linda tortured the kids without hesitation. Amber was balancing on a thin line between killing Mrs. Linda and killing herself. It had gotten to the point where both of those ideas seemed reasonable. But Amber couldn't act on that thought. She knew that her spy cameras would arrive that day and she could finally capture Mrs. Linda and expose her for the evil bitch that she has become. Five o'clock rolled around and Amber

Tony D. Gunn Jr.

knew that the delivery man, Mr. Andre, would be arriving anytime now.

She wondered how she would make it outside to get the package without Mrs. Linda knowing. Then, she had an idea, but it would come with a price. After going to the bathroom, she went upstairs to ask Robert something.

"Robert, I really need your help." stated Amber.

Robert turned his head toward Amber and appeared to be engaged in the conversation.

"I need you to ask mama if we can get some ice cream." said Amber.

Amber didn't really want any ice cream. She just needed Robert to do that so all of Mrs. Linda's attention would be on him and she could get her order, even if that distraction turned into a beating for Robert. Amber knew that risking her brother's safety was the only way she would have a chance to retrieve her order without getting caught. But it was the fastest way at the moment. Robert didn't realize, yet, what Amber was doing so he concurred. Amber told Robert to make sure he was all the way by the back door when he asked for the ice cream. Amber watched out the window for Mr. Andre and his delivery truck.

Tony D. Gunn Jr.

She saw the truck coming down the street and told Robert that it was time to ask Mrs. Linda because she was doing the dishes and already in the kitchen. Robert and Amber went down the stairs; Amber went to the front door and Robert headed for the kitchen. Then she hurried and went onto the front porch. Mr. Andre had just started to walk up the sidewalk to the house.

"Hey, sunshine!" said Mr. Andre.

"Good afternoon, Mr. Andre." said Amber with a slight smile on her face.

"I have a package for you, but is your mom here?" asked Mr. Andre.

Amber had a thought in her head to panic, but she decided not to tell the truth for the safety of her own wellbeing.

"She's busy cleaning the basement; would you like for me to get her?" asked Amber even though she wasn't going to do that.

"Naw, it's okay. I trust you. You just be good and enjoy your break." said Mr. Andre as he handed Amber the package.

"I sure will!" replied Amber.

Tony D. Gunn Jr.

Amber ran into the house with the package and heard Robert being beaten by Mrs. Linda. She ran straight upstairs to her room and opened the package. A sly smile appeared at the sight of the brand new spy cameras that could potentially save their lives.

Amber was good at following instructions. Every since she was six years old, she could assemble her own toys just by looking at the pictures on the instructions. After she read the instructions, she started to place the cameras everywhere that was currently Mom-free while she was occupied with Robert. She put one in the bathroom, the hallway, the two bedrooms, the computer room, and even two on the balcony, one to watch the balcony and one to look down into the backyard.

When the installation of the spy cameras was finished upstairs, she went in her room and found Robert in tears under his covers. He was curled up and hurting from his beating. Amber told Robert that she was sorry for what had happened to him. She told him that maybe they would get ice cream when Darnell got home because that seemed to be the only time Mrs. Linda didn't beat them. She wanted to tell why she asked him to do her a favor, but she knew that would jeopardize what she was doing.

Tony D. Gunn Jr.

Chapter 10

Meanwhile downstairs, Mrs. Linda had noticed Mr. Andre's delivery truck outside her house and invited him in for a drink. He politely thanked her and declined, but she insisted. Mr. Andre knew that going into the house was jeopardizing his job. So, Mr. Andre accepted the free drink, besides, he couldn't resist the urge. Mrs. Linda and Mr. Andre sat in the living room lightly drinking and engaging in a conversation. Time passed and finally Mr. Andre said he had to finish his route. He thanked her for the drink and started to get up from off of the couch until Mrs. Linda hopped up on him and started to kiss him.

Tony D. Gunn Jr.

They fell onto the couch and Mr. Andre tried to stop her from doing that, but the emotional appeal overweighed the idea of her having a husband and it also overweighed her having a family. He took off his shirt and grabbed her buttocks. The passion between them looked as if they were in love for years. It look as if they were married and about to make love to each other again, but in reality, they were about to fornicate.

Mrs. Linda insisted that they finished what she started upstairs in her room, but Mr. Andre was worried about the kids hearing. Mrs. Linda told him that the kids were sound asleep and the TV was on to suffocate the sounds they would make. Mr. Andre picked her up and ran up the stairs into her bedroom. He sat her on the bed and closed the door.

The kids sat in their room completely unaware of the adultery that was occurring just one room away. All Amber knew was that she heard somebody go into her parents' room and suspected it was Mrs. Linda, so she took that opportunity to install the rest of her spy cameras all around the house. When she was finished, she went back to her room.

Tony D. Gunn Jr.

A half hour later Mr. Andre was back on his route and the family was waiting for Darnell to get home. Having lost time with her afternoon's activity, Mrs. Linda started dinner late. When Darnell arrived home he was greeted by his family. As he looked at Mrs. Linda, he had flashbacks of their argument before her accident. He got his mind off that horrible memory and got the kids so he and they could all watch a movie in the living room 'til Mrs. Linda finished dinner. An hour passed and dinner was finally ready.

"Dinner's ready!" yelled Mrs. Linda as she sat the last steak on Darnell's plate.

They went into the kitchen and began eating dinner. While Amber was eating, she realized they hadn't blessed their food in a long time. She started to ask Darnell if she could say grace, but she decided to just go ahead and say it:

"My Lord, we want to thank you for allowing us the opportunity to eat this meal. We hope that you take all the negative things out of this house and put in positive. Lord may your blessings pour over our food as we fill our bellies. In Jesus name, we pray, Amen." recited Amber.

"Amen" said Darnell.

"Amen" said Bobby.

Tony D. Gunn Jr.

"Amen." said Mrs. Linda.

They all finished eating then headed to their rooms because, with the late dinner, it was time for bed. After awhile, she went to sleep with a smile on her face.

Chapter 11

For the next five weeks, Mrs. Linda was torturing the kids. Darnell noticed a bruise on Robert, but it was small and Mrs. Linda sure had a cover up. The good thing about it, though, was that Amber was capturing it all on camera. Those days were the worst days of their lives, but what they didn't know was there were more of them to come.

On the sixth week that the cameras have been running, they were about to catch something unforeseen. On Tuesday, the morning started as usual; they ate breakfast and Darnell went to work. The children were back into their room before Darnell left out and Mrs. Linda was washing the dishes. Mrs. Linda went under the sink and got an empty spray bottle. She filled it with water and called Robert downstairs.

"I want you to go water the plants in the backyard and on the balcony." said Mrs. Linda.

Robert grabbed the spray bottle and did it with no hesitation. He went to do the plants in the backyard first since he was already downstairs. He watered each one carefully and he actually enjoyed it. This was the first time in a long time that he had a sincere smile on his face. When he finished watering the plants in the backyard, he headed to the balcony. There were four plants on the balcony: two sitting on the railing post and two that extended from the balcony and dangled over the backyard.

He watered the two plants that were easy then was thrilled to see that he had a challenge. He was a short little fellow and his arm span couldn't reach the two plants that dangled over the backyard. He struggled and extended his arm as much as he could, but he realized that wasn't enough. So he grabbed the milk crate that was on the balcony and stood up on it. Leaning toward the first dangling plant, Robert was able to reach it with no problem. Then he got down from the milk crate and scooted it over, so that he can try to water the other dangling plant.

He leant over to water the plant when all of a sudden he felt his feet come up from the milk crate and his body spiraling towards the ground. It all happened so fast that Robert didn't have time to think what to do. "Boom, Crack!" His body was lying on the ground with his head on backwards; motionless, breathless, disfigured...dead! The spray bottle lay beside Robert as if it decided to take that journey with Robert. Amber heard the thump as she was coming down the stairs, so she ran toward the backyard. She opened the door and saw Robert lying there.

"Robert! Robert!" cried Amber.

She ran over to him and crouched down over him. Tears dripped from Amber's face onto Robert's back. Mrs. Linda came out the house a few seconds later, walked over to Bobby, and dropped down to her knees.

As she pulled Amber off Robert, she said, "You must be strong. This accident was tragic, but you must learn how to live with no worries and prepare for the worse."

Tony D. Gunn Jr.

Amber looked up at Mrs. Linda and said "You did this! You did it!"

Mrs. Linda grabbed Amber by her hair and dragged her into the house. "Flop!" Amber was tossed onto the couch. "If I would have pushed anybody off the balcony, it would have been you. He was supposed to water the plants. I guess he couldn't handle it!" yelled Mrs. Linda as she ended the conversation with a smack. Amber ran upstairs to her room and hopped in her bed. She couldn't believe that her only brother was dead. Her only friend was dead. And she thought it was all her fault.

"I know she did it. She had to. Robert would never take his own life or even fail a physical challenge that little." though Amber as she went to retrieve the memory card out the balcony cameras.

Tony D. Gunn Jr.

Chapter 12

Meanwhile, Mrs. Linda was on the phone with the police. She called them crying about how Robert had an accident and that he was too young to die. Once the phone conversation ended with the police, she pulled the same fake crying on Darnell. Darnell speeded down the highway toward his home. All while driving he kept having flashbacks of when he raced to the hospital for Mrs. Linda. His thoughts were interrupted by the sirens of a patrol car. The officer was trying to pull Darnell over for speeding, but Darnell didn't stop. He floored it and managed to lead the officer straight to his house.

Tony D. Gunn Jr.

This was tangible because all the nearby patrol cars all responded to the call from Darnell's house. The block was full of police and ambulance by the time Darnell explained to the officer that was pursuing him. Amber and Mrs. Linda ran out the house in tears, straight into Darnell's arms. The officers and Darnell believed every bit of lie that Mrs. Linda spit out her mouth, but Amber still had a feeling it wasn't an accident. She had not had a chance to watch the video that was on the memory card, but she was certain someone will.

Once the authorities processed the scene and cleaned it up, the family sat in the living room trying to decide how to deal with this. Darnell immediately called off from work, so that he could spend every second with his incomplete family. Spend every second with his hurting family. Three hurting faces sat in the living room, but only two of those were sincere. Darnell started to talk to Amber and calm her down. He understood that this incident must have really hurt her because it hurt him more. He went on-and-on about how everything would be okay.

Then Amber asked to be excused. She told him that she wanted to go lay down. Darnell gave her permission to and she went upstairs. Mrs. Linda and Darnell continued to talk

Tony D. Gunn Jr.

about what happened. She told Darnell that it was all her fault because if she would have never told him to water the plants then he would still be here.

"It's not your fault, baby. There's no way you could have known he was going to fall. Just stop beating yourself up and go upstairs and get some rest." said Darnell as he hugged Mrs. Linda so dearly.

Mrs., Linda headed upstairs and Darnell stayed there on the couch thinking about the incident.

"A detective will surely be coming by anytime now and if you say a word about what I did to you or Bobby, I will kill all of you." said Mrs. Linda as she entered Amber's room.

Amber nodded her head then lay down as if she had been tired. She was too anxious to retrieve the rest of the spy cameras. Amber waited 'til Mrs. Linda and Darnell were in their room to get the memory cards out of the other cameras. Once she got them, she put a backup copy onto the desk top inside a folder that was in hundreds of other folders. She did this so that it would not be easily identified just by looking at the main screen.

Tony D. Gunn Jr.

She wanted to watch the videos, but she knew that it would take too long to find the right clip and she would get caught. Once finished, she went to her room and went to sleep. Eleven a.m. sharp, Detective Foreman was at their house questioning them. He individually questioned Darnell, then Mrs. Linda, then Amber. When it was Amber's turn, she told Detective Foreman that she didn't see anything or know anything at first. But when he was just about to conclude the conversation, Amber hand him the memory cards.

"Please, don't say a word about this to my parents. Just watch them, please!" whispered Amber as she started to cry.

Detective Foreman hugged Amber to comfort her and promised he wouldn't open his mouth about it. Once Detective Foreman left, the family continued to talk in the living room about what to do next. Darnell stated that he already started to make the funeral arrangements. He also expressed that he knows how much they all loved Robert, but his unfortunate encounter couldn't cause constant sadness within this household because that's not what Robert would have wanted. The family agreed to what Darnell had to say just like they always did.

Tony D. Gunn Jr.

They sat around up under each other the rest of the afternoon watching TV. But they were unaware of what Detective Foreman was watching. He and his partner, Detective Christian, had been looking over the videos for hours and were perturbed. They saw that Robert's death wasn't an accident, he was killed! The video showed Mrs. Linda pulling the milk crate from under Robert and her starring viciously at his dead body on the ground.

Detective Foreman felt abashed because he should have known that it wasn't an accident. He had gotten a bad vibe when he was talking with Mrs. Linda, but he just let her crying appearance overwrite his thoughts. Detective Christian took the videos to District Attorney Adam and pleaded him to put that tape on top of everything else he was working on. She did this because she knew that Amber was still in danger.

"We can go watch the tapes now." said District Attorney Adam as he pointed to his office.

They watched the tapes and he told the detectives there was enough evidence for an arrest. So District Attorney Adam rushed an Arrest Warrant from Judge Davis and gave it to the officers. Sirens yelled through the city of Atlanta, GA. Police car after police car pulled in front of the

Brown's home. The family heard the commotion outside and wondered what it was. The window blinds split and three set of eyes layered them. When Mrs. Linda realized what was happening, she quietly tip-toed away and grabbed the baseball bat out the closet.

"Bam! Bam!" Mrs. Linda struck Darnell and Amber in the back of their head. Instantly, Amber and Darnell were unconsciously lying on the floor. Mrs. Linda ran upstairs and grabbed the gun Darnell kept in a wall safe. When she ran back down the stairs, she noticed some police officers knocking on the door.

"This is the police. Open this door or we will gain entrance by force!" yelled Detective Foreman.

Tony D. Gunn Jr.

Chapter 13

Mrs. Linda cocked the gun back and fire five shots through the door. Officers scattered off of the porch and took cover behind their cars. She ran into the living room and opened the blinds all the way up. The motion immediately got the attention of the officers. They all looked at the window as the S.W.A.T. team had arrived on the scene. Mrs. Linda propped the two bodies on the window and pushed the couch behind them so they wouldn't fall.

Detective Foreman turned on the Blow Horn and said, "You don't want to do this. Just calm down, we are only here to ask you some questions."

Mrs. Linda pulled the couch from propping them and they fell onto the living room floor. She closed the blinds aggressively and sat on the couch. She sat there thinking about what she should do next. There was no turning back from this point. Everything that happened was out in the open. And when this thought came across her mind, she got up off the couch and walked over to Amber. "Pow!"

She started *to* pistol whoop Amber over and over while saying, "You did this. You did this!"

As she did this, the S.W.A.T. team was on their way in through the back door. Mrs. Linda didn't notice the intruders. She was too caught up in beating Amber's already unconscious body.

"Freeze!" yelled Detective Christian.

Mrs. Linda turned around to nine guns pointed to her face.

"Ha Ha Ha, You think this is over." said Mrs. Linda as she dropped the gun and put her hands on her head.

Detective Foreman took charge and put the handcuffs on Mrs. Linda.

"You have the right to remain silent. Anything you do or say can and will be used against you in the court of law. You have the right to an attorney. If you cannot afford one,

one will be appointed to you." stated Detective Foreman as he walked Mrs. Linda out the house.

Detective Christian checked Darnell and Amber for a pulse just as the paramedics were entering the *h*ouse. A pulse was present on both of them so the paramedics put them on stretchers and escorted them to the hospital. Hours passed when Darnell finally woke up. His body was ached with pain, but his mind ached more.

"My baby! My baby! Doc, where is my daughter?" cried Darnell.

"Calm down, Mr. Darnell. Amber is getting treated and will be in recovery soon from the unconscious state as we speak." explained Dr. John.

Darnell lay back on the bed and began to ask the doctor what happened. The doctor informs him that he was knocked unconscious by a blunt object. He also told Darnell that Detectives Foreman and Christian would arrive any minute now to inform you more. And sure enough, they arrived a few minutes later. They went over with Darnell about what happened at the house.

Darnell was shocked and con*f*used about why Mrs. Linda would have done that. And he was even more confused as

Tony D. Gunn Jr.

to why they were there to get her in the first place. They showed Darnell edited versions of the videos; the videos were clipped to the points that showed action. When Darnell watched the first beating caught on tape he instantly started to cry. Tears had never come out of his eyes in such numbers. He couldn't believe what his eyes were seeing. Then the policed warned him of what he was about to see next. They showed Darnell the tape of when Mrs. Linda killed Bobby. Darnell cried out even louder.

"Where is she? I'm going to kill that heifer...I hope she rots in hell!" yelled Darnell as he attempted to get out of bed.

Detective Foreman calmed him down and told him that Mrs. Linda was in their custody. Darnell went on-and-on about how dumb he was for not noticing his kids getting beat while he was gone. Then it all started to come to him. He started to have flashbacks of situations when the kids acted completely unusual.

He felt like a failure to his kids. He was supposed to protect them, instead he let a women torture them both and kill one. Dr. John walked in and informed both the detectives and Darnell that Amber has been woke for five minutes now and she is stable. The Detectives asked

Darnell if they could talk to her and Darnell said yes, but he wanted to be present. He didn't have a problem with them talking to her alone, but he just didn't want Amber to have to say everything more than once.

Darnell slowly got up off the bed and the doctor tried to tell him to rest, but he refused. All three of them walked to the room that held Amber. As soon as Amber got in Darnell's sight, he ran over to her and held her in his arms. They exchanged kisses and hugs. Then Darnell started to talk about how sorry he was that he didn't notice what was going on. He promised Amber that he would never let that happen again. Amber started to cry and begged Darnell to stop crying.

She told him that she was sorry for keeping it all bottled inside and that if she would have said something sooner then maybe Robert would still be alive.

"Don't think like that!" yelled Darnell, "I'm sorry for yelling baby, but please stop that. You had no choice. She probably would have killed us all if you would have said something."

Amber dropped her head with tears dripping into her lap.

Tony D. Gunn Jr.

"Now these officers want to talk to you baby. Try your best to answer everything as best as you can." said Darnell.

"Hey Amber, I'm Detective Foreman and this is my partner Detective Christian." said Detective Foreman.

They started to ask Amber questions regarding how long the torturing has been going on and to what extent. They took notes as she spoke about it. After about a half hour, the questioning stopped and the Detectives had all they needed. They left the hospital. It was time to return to the station, put all the evidence together, and make a case against Mrs. Linda. Dr. John released Amber and Darnell the next morning. Both of them were stilled bruised physically and mentally.

Their tangible family went from four to two and that didn't sit well with them. The same thoughts ran across Darnell's mind. "Where do we go from here? What am I going to do now?"

They decided to check into a hotel. They did this because they didn't want to step foot into that house again. It hosted too many bad memories and regrets. It was best for them to leave it alone for now.

Chapter 14

Meanwhile, back at the police station, the Detectives were getting everything ready for the pre trial hearing. They had solid evidence: videos of torture, a video of murder, and victim statements that corresponded. All they were waiting on was a court date.

Bail was set at a million. "Whew!" responded Detective Christian. The tables were truly turning now. As Mrs. Linda was carted out of the court room, she was already thinking of her master plan. Officer Travis proudly escorted her to her cell. He was happy about it because it was his 200th escort and he was more proud to be putting away such a bad woman. Mrs. Linda eyes rolled to the back of her head as those cold, hard bars slammed shut.

Tony D. Gunn Jr.

"What's up, Shorty?" said Deliya.

Deliya was an inmate and she was in prison for soliciting her two year old girl and killing her pimp. Mrs. Linda didn't reply to Deliya. Deliya said a few bad words to Mrs. Linda then hopped on the top bunk. For the next six weeks, Mrs. Linda sat in the same spot on the floor just thinking of her master plan. She only moved when a prison officer forced her to. She didn't talk to no one, she didn't make any friends, and she didn't even blink half the time.

Her main focus was on her plan. She had finally thought of what she was going to do. Little at a time, Mrs. Linda started to scrap off the paint on the prison wall. She didn't stop scrapping until she thought she had enough; enough to get her ill. She threw the paint scrapings into her mouth and swallowed it. A couple hours passed and she was throwing up all over the cell.

Deliya called her all types of names, to the point that Mrs. Linda had enough. She grabbed Deliya by the throat and slammed her onto the floor. As Deliya gasped for air she left her mouth wide open. Mrs. Linda vomited in Deliya's mouth then laughed at her and told her to shut up. When Mrs. Linda released Deliya, she spit out the vomit and started to wash out her mouth in the sink.

Tony D. Gunn Jr.

When the guards finally arrived, Mrs. Linda was on the floor lying in her own vomit. They picked her up and took her to the prison nurse. The nurse informed them that Mrs. Linda would need to go to a hospital to be diagnosed and carefully treated for this illness. Officer Grant escorted Mrs. Linda to a hospital and he was appointed to take position by the door. When Mrs. Linda got to the hospital, Dr. Christian took some of Mrs. Linda's blood to run test.

When Dr. Christian realized the problem and treated Mrs. Linda, he told her that he would let her stay a little while longer to recover from the illness. She sat in the hospital room alone. Only person nearby was Officer Grant and he was on the other side of the door.

"Excuse me, Officer!" yelled Mrs. Linda.

Officer Grant entered the room and went over to the side of her bed.

"How may I help you?" said Officer Grant.

"Can you come a little closer? It hurts to talk loudly." asked Mrs. Linda.

Officer Grant bent over and came inches from Mrs. Linda's face.

Tony D. Gunn Jr.

Mrs. Linda whispered, "I want you!" as she pulled Officer Grant's head to hear lips and started to kiss his ears.

Officer Grant pulled up and said, "You know we can't do this. If I get caught, I could lose my job."

"Who said anything about getting caught?" said Mrs. Linda as she pulled him down on to her.

Officer Grant was so overtook by her appearance that he gave in to lust! His mind was telling him no, but his body was telling him yes! The appeal he got from the thought of it at that moment felt like nothing he had ever experienced. While tranquilized in thought, Mrs. Linda slipped the handcuff key from off of his pants and un-cuffed herself. She flipped Officer Grant over and rapidly got on top of him. She started taking off the rest of Officer Grant's clothes with her teeth, piece-by-piece; and then the clothes fell to the floor.

Officer Grant started to feel a little vulnerable, but he stopped worrying the more she kissed on him. Then she tied a sheet covering his mouth and the back of his head so that he could not talk to loud. "Swoosh!" She stabbed an IV into Officer Grant's arm and the bad thing was...she was

Tony D. Gunn Jr.

pumping air into his veins. She climbed off of him and walked over to the sink and mirror.

"Slash! Slash!" Mrs. Linda begin cutting off all her hair. Hair fell to the floor as if it was attracted to it. Finally, Mrs. Linda was done cutting her hair, she picked up Officer Grant's uniform and looked at him. Tears rolled down his face as he started to feel the pain of the vein erupting inside of him. She put on his uniform and made sure it looked sharp. She was going to pose as Officer Grant. She kissed Officer Grant as she unlocked one of the handcuffs.

"You might want to hit that 'Doctor Alert' button if you want to stay alive." said Mrs. Linda as she walked out the door.

And just like that, Mrs. Linda was gone. Officer Grant hit the button as fast as he could. He was scared of dying and he almost panicked himself to death. Dr. Christian and Nurse Monae ran into the room. They were shocked to see Officer Grant handcuffed to the bed with an IV in him.

"She escaped!" yelled Officer Grant as he fainted. "Go tell security to lock the building down now!" yelled Dr. Christian.

Tony D. Gunn Jr.

As Nurse Monae ran to follow her orders, Dr. Christian ran over to Officer Grant. He tried to do everything he could, but he noticed the IV erupted his main vein. There was no hope for Officer Grant. Dr. Christian removed the IV needle from Officer Grant's arm and dropped his head. She was ashamed that this occurred with his presence in this hospital. Meanwhile, security was locking the building and searching all over for Mrs. Linda, but what they didn't know was she was already gone.

By the time the doctor and nurse realized the alert button was ringing, Mrs. Linda was walking off the hospital parking lot. They searched and searched, but they never found Mrs. Linda in that hospital. Dr. Christian contacted the prison ward and informed her of what occurred. The prison ward was furious and asked Dr. Christian how could she let this happen.

But Dr. Christian wasn't having it. She yelled right back at the prison ward stating that she assigned an officer to stand guard at Mrs. Linda's door. She said that she should teach her workers how to be in a close encounter with dangerous women. After a heated argument, Dr. Christian realized that wasn't going to bring Officer Grant back or bring Mrs. Linda back in custody. She told her that her

Tony D. Gunn Jr.

main focus should be on catching Mrs. Linda before she kills again.

Tony D. Gunn Jr.

Chapter 15

Darnell's cell phone rang as he and Amber were watching one of their favorite movies.

"Hello?" said Darnell.

"Good afternoon, am I speaking with Darnell Brown?" said Detective Foreman.

"Yes, this is him." replied Darnell.

"This is Detective Foreman. I was calling to ask you if anything suspicious had happened these past few hours?" asked Detective Foreman.

"No. Why you ask that?" said Darnell.

Tony D. Gunn Jr.

Darnell's mind started to detach from the movie and Amber. He was curious about the call. In all honesty, Darnell was scared about the call.

"Well, there's been a situation down at the hospital." said Detective Foreman.

"The hospital?" thought Darnell.

He began to get confused about the call. He knew nothing about someone being in the hospital.

"Who was in the hospital?" asked Darnell.

"Mrs. Linda was transported to the hospital a day ago for an illness and...She escaped!" said Detective Foreman.

Darnell immediately got up off the bed and went into the bathroom.

"She escaped! What do you mean she escaped? How does a women escape? I know you all had officers appointed to watch her!" said Darnell.

"Sir, that is true. We did have an officer assigned to watch her, but he was killed." said Detective Foreman.

Tony D. Gunn Jr.

Darnell face turned pale as he peeked around the corner and starred at Amber. He knew that if Amber found out that Mrs. Linda was free, she would be terrified.

"This has all been one bad dream! I just watched them put my son in the ground five days ago. I had to watch tears fall from my little girl's eyes! And now to tell me that the person who put my son in the ground is free...it just...it just sickens me! So what should we do?" said Darnell.

"Did you all plan on going back to that house?" asked Detective Foreman.

"No. I was planning on starting fresh in about a month or two. I didn't want to remind my little girl of all the things she had to endure." replied Darnell.

"Okay, good. That's a start. There should be no way for Mrs. Linda to know where you are. We will have a patrol car sitting outside the hotel at all time. We will catch her!" said Detective Foreman.

The conversation continued for about five more minutes before Darnell decided he was done talking. He went back into the room where Amber was watching TV.

Tony D. Gunn Jr.

"Who was that, daddy?" asked Amber.

"Oh baby, that was somebody who had the wrong number." said Darnell.

Darnell didn't want to lie to her, but he had no choice. He must sacrifice his word for his daughter's well being. That night Darnell kept Amber in his sight the entire time. He went into the hallway to look down both ends and make sure nothing suspicious was happening.

He check outside the hotel windows to make sure Mrs. Linda wasn't climbing up the side of the hotel. He didn't underestimate Mrs. Linda at all. Eventually he fell asleep with Amber in his arms. Morning time rolled around and Darnell was awakened by a brief breeze dancing across his chin. First he noticed the window open, and then he noticed the top of a ladder sticking into the window. Darnell turn his head to the right and there she was. Mrs. Linda held Amber by her hair and a gun in her mouth. Tears were already draining from Amber's eyes.

"Please don't do this!" said Darnell as he got up slowly.

"Don't come any closer! I'll blow her head off!" yelled Mrs. Linda.

"No, no, please!" said Darnell, "why are you doing this?"

"Ha! Why am I doing this? You want to know why I am doing this. There are always consequences for what a person wishes for." said Mrs. Linda as she cocked the gun back and stuck it back into Amber's mouth.

"Baby, please don't do this!" said Darnell.

"Oh, so now I'm your baby?" said Mrs. Linda.

"Yes, baby. You don't have to do this!" said Darnell.

Mrs. Linda wasn't fazed by the words that came out of Darnell's mouth, but she wanted to see where he was going with it; she wanted to entertain his ignorance.

"Baby, put the gun down. I'm sorry for making you feel unwanted. We can be a happy family." said Darnell as tears continued to roll down his face.

Mrs. Linda took the gun out of Amber's mouth and placed it on the dresser. She started to fake cry about how sorry she was as she released Amber. Darnell walked over to her and as soon as he got close to her, he leaped for the gun. Mrs. Linda tried to grab the gun too, but Darnell was too

Tony D. Gunn Jr.

fast. "Boom!" A bullet pierced Mrs. Linda's throat. She fell to the ground, blood everywhere.

Mrs. Linda's eyes closed and all her muscles loosened; she was dead! Darnell dropped to his knees and Amber ran over to hug him. They sat there crying on the floor. Their minds were overloaded with horrible events, but in all, they were glad to be alive. Sirens roared all around them and it felt like an enormous weight was lifted off their shoulders. It was finally over, or so they thought!

Tony D. Gunn Jr.

Tony D. Gunn Jr.

I've learned that a person can take something out of everything they read or do. That 'thing' is the moral of it.

The moral of "The Collateral Soul":

Lies within the text.

Only the Eyes of the Wise Will Be Able to Discover the Moral that's in Disguise.

4/8/2/4/3/7/2/4/2/2/6/6/2/6/4/8/2/3

Quoted by Tony D. Gunn Jr.

Tony D. Gunn Jr.

About The Author

Tony D. Gunn Jr. was born in St. Louis, Mo. He started his writing in the 8th grade in 2009, in which was the work behind his first book, "The Erratic Regret". He began writing this book, "The Collateral Soul", in January, 2012He has dedicated long, hard hours to this book, but he also had to learn. And the only way for him to learn was to read! The author that influenced him the most was Gary Paulsen. He used to read the Brain Series by Gary Paulsen and it really helped him build his vocabulary. During the work behind this book, Tony read a very popular and amazing magazine titled, "The SUN Magazine". Although this is his 2nd book in 5 years, he states that his hand repels to stop writing. He's a man of diversity, so he will have his readers encounter many different genre of books. Writing has not only given Tony the opportunity to express himself, it provided him with something to engage in other than running a mockery around town. Tony, 18, is an Honors Graduate from Clyde C. Miller Career Academy. He was awarded the "Best Speaker Award of the Class of 2014" due to his excellent communication skills amongst his peers. He takes his work seriously and understands what it means to "stand out from others."

The Collateral Soul

Tony D. Gunn Jr.

Tony D. Gunn Jr.